Your
Brave Song

illustrated by Amy Grimes

ANN VOSKAMP
New York Times Bestselling Author

Tyndale House Publishers
Carol Stream, Illinois

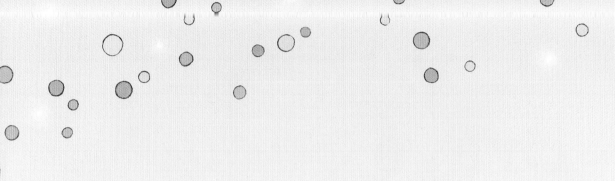

Visit Tyndale's website for kids at tyndale.com/kids.

Visit the author's website at annvoskamp.com.

Tyndale is a registered trademark of Tyndale House Ministries. The Tyndale Kids logo is a trademark of Tyndale House Ministries.

Your Brave Song

Designed by Jacqueline L. Nuñez

Edited by Stephanie Rische

Published in association with William K. Jensen Literary Agency, 119 Bampton Court, Eugene, Oregon 97404.

For manufacturing information regarding this product, please call 1-855-277-9400.

For information about special discounts for bulk purchases, please contact Tyndale House Publishers at csresponse@tyndale.com, or call 1-855-277-9400.

Library of Congress Cataloging-in-Publication Data

A catalog record for this book is available from the Library of Congress.

ISBN 978-1-4964-4654-1

Printed in China

29	28	27	26	25	24	23
7	6	5	4	3	2	1

Una Rayne stood on the front steps with her mama,
looking out at a morning fog thick enough
you could almost scoop it with a spoon.

Una Rayne could barely see
her hands in front of her face.

She could barely see
the tips of her boots.

She could barely see her face
in the puddles at her feet.

2

She could barely see her way forward
any which way at all.

Before Una Rayne
could even tuck her tiny hand
into her mama's hand, her mama slipped down
next to her and gently gathered her up into her lap.
She wrapped her in a hug as warm as the sun
that's always shining way
above the fog and clouds.

4

"You have big places to go
and all kinds of big things ahead of you,"
her mama said. "You may feel small
and not sure of the way at all." Mama murmured
what Una Rayne was thinking, the way
mamas can sometimes
read your heart like an open story book.

"But right here inside of you?" Mama tapped
on Una Rayne's chest like she was knocking on the door
of her heart. "In here lives the biggest and greatest song.
The one that makes you brave."

As Una Rayne picked up
her backpack and stepped off
the porch into her
big day of big things, her mama
sang softly after her. And those words
blew like a warming breeze
all around Una Rayne.

7

Jesus loves you,
Makes you strong.
In Him you're brave
And you belong.

8

And that one little string of words
made a path through the fog,
and the gray soup of clouds lifted.

Suddenly Una Rayne could
see her way forward, one big,
brave step after another.

9

With every puddle she leaped over,
Una Rayne looked down and saw all of herself.

And when you see who you really are,
and you see how Jesus loves you just as you are,
and how He loves you enough to change
and grow how you are—

that's when you can see
how safe in His love you really are,
no matter where you are.

So she sang it
with every big,
brave leap:

Jesus loves you,
Makes you strong.
In Him you're brave
And you belong.

11

But when it was time
for Una Rayne to find a seat
at lunch on her big day in a
big new place, she couldn't find
any place at any table just for her.

She couldn't find a place with the big kids
with all their big hair. She couldn't find
a place with all the little kids
with all their little toys.

She couldn't find a place to squeeze in
with any of the kids at all.

But somewhere
deep inside of
Una Rayne, there was
that place that had
made space for the
song that makes
you brave.

14

And that song, when she sang it strong and loud,
made space for Una Rayne to stretch her arms wide open:

Jesus loves you,
Makes you strong.
In Him you're brave
And you belong.

15

And that one little string of words
pulled the happiest plan together.
Una Rayne smiled her surest smile
and flung her jacket down on the grass.
And then she set out her nuts and
her slices of apples and her cheese.

16

And before long, the squirrels scampered round

The birds swooped down.

The ducks sauntered up.

And a little kid and a big kid and
a kid just Una Rayne's size sat down beside her.

And Una Rayne found out
there is always a place that wants you—
if you're brave enough to make that space
by making space in your world
for them to be with you.

So Una Rayne passed around her cookies and sang
to every single person gathered around,
only this time she wasn't singing alone.
She smiled big and helped everyone learn the words
themselves, so they all sang along:

Jesus loves you,
Makes you strong.
In Him you're brave
And you belong.

And when Una Rayne crawled into bed that night
after her big day in a big new place,
she pulled the covers up close and felt how her blankets
wrapped around her like the longest hug.

22

She knew there would be days
when hard winds would
blow her backward.

There would be days
when she would step in puddles
up to her knees.

There would be days
when the special, tender parts
of her one brave heart
would get hurt.

But on those days, there was a bigger song
within her that was louder than any lies,
a song that was stronger
than any sadness. And Una Rayne
sang it back to the world
every night like a gift.

24

Jesus loves you,
Makes you strong.
In Him you're brave
And you belong.

25

And that one little string of words ties
all the brave hearts to Jesus, who is Love Himself. And His whisper
beats inside our hearts: "You are chosen, not for what you do,
but for who you are. For *whose* you are."

26

Una Rayne looked out the window. All the fog had cleared,
revealing an endless blanket of blinking stars . . .
each one made by God, chosen by God,
named by God. And those stars couldn't stop
singing and twinkle-dancing with the glory of it.

Jesus loves you,
Makes you strong.
In Him you're brave
And you belong.

And the words ring all through the world, like a heavenly song that is from
far beyond this world—the song that is the very heartbeat of Love Himself.
It's always His perfect love for you, which goes endlessly on and on,
which fills your heart with the very bravest song.

Glue
your child's
photo here.

The LORD your God . . . is always with you.
He celebrates and sings because of you, and
he will refresh your life with his love.

Zephaniah 3:17, CEV